THE
PROUD CHICKEN

WRITTEN BY MIKE JOENS
ILLUSTRATED BY LEN SIMON

A Whitestone Media Little Overhill Book™

Theo Cottage Illustration by Mike Hodgson
Book Layout by Brandon Joens

First Edition Printed in U.S.A. by Worzalla, February 2015

ISBN: 978-0-9906118-1-3

From Mike to Patti & Gary Hathaway
From Len to Charlie & Cooper

www.theopresents.com

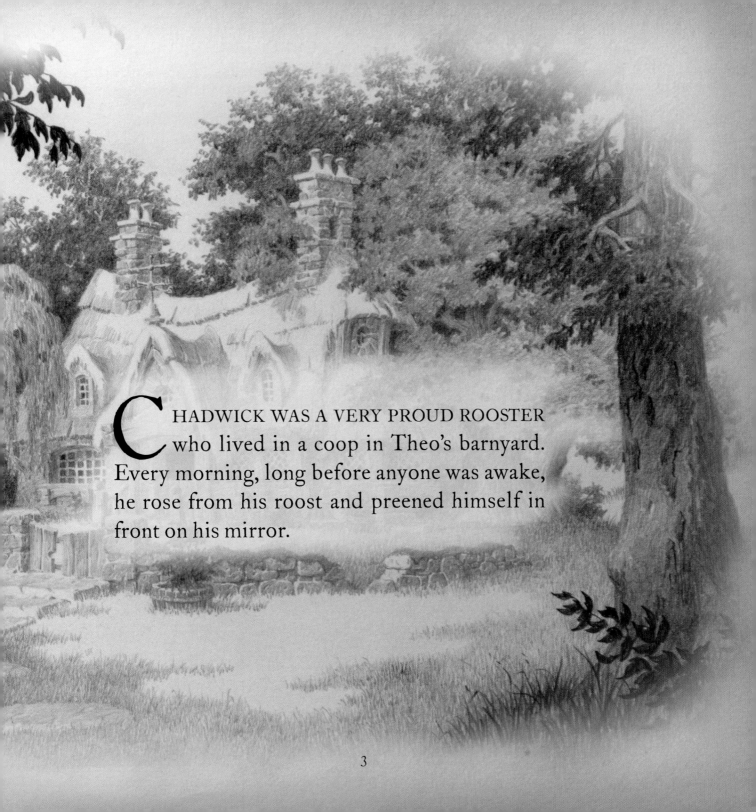

CHADWICK WAS A VERY PROUD ROOSTER who lived in a coop in Theo's barnyard. Every morning, long before anyone was awake, he rose from his roost and preened himself in front on his mirror.

Strutting back and forth to view his feathers from every angle, clicked his tongue and said, "Chadwick, my dear fellow, you certainly are a handsome rooster."

Afterward he paraded among the hens sleeping on their nests, and said with a proud swish of his tail feathers, "Good morning, my dears. Don't you think my feathers are the most beautiful in the world?"

"You certainly think so," the hens muttered under their breath.

Unaware of their scorn, Chadwick flew up to the top of the barn, cleared his throat and sang, "So Sweet the Sunrise."

"SO SWE-E-E-ET THE MORNING BREAKS FAIR LI-IG-I-I-I-HT...!!!"

"Aaaaiieeeeee...not again!!!" the animals in Theo's barnyard howled.

"...ITS GOLDEN BEAMS FROM LOFTY HE-E-E-IGHT..."

Monty the draft horse bucked and snorted, and nearly kicked down his stall. Oscar the goat butted the side of the barn and knocked boards loose. The hens cackled and squawked and sent feathers flying, shouting, "One simply cannot lay eggs with all that braying!"

Every morning it was the same.

Chadwick lifted his beak in a haughty manner and said, "Fiddlesticks." But on this fair morning, he added, "Since none of you appreciate my fine voice, perhaps I shall leave."

The animals shouted, "*PLEASE LEAVE!*"

"I shall," said Chadwick. And with a flick of his wattle, and a swish of his tail feathers, he strutted down the lane to show the world what a truly great rooster he was.

As Chadwick made his way along the country lane, he composed wonderful songs—a *Lullaby for a Lily*, a *Ballad for a Bumblebee*. Sadly, there was no one around to hear him sing. For whenever he came near, not a single woodland creature could be found.

The proud rooster couldn't understand why.

Later, as he crested the hill overlooking the village of Little Overhill, he heard the sweet sound of music. Chadwick flew quickly to its source.

Nestled in a shady dell, where the greenwood crept along the edge of the village, was a watery nook called Pollywog Pond. On this golden morning, a knot of toads was throwing a birthday party for Old Thaddeus the bull toad, and their voices filled the air with joyous toad-song.

"Finally an audience to appreciate my fine voice," Chadwick, thought. "I shall compose a moving melody, and call it "*Ode to Toads.*" "WITH BIRTHDAY CHEERS TO TOADS SO DE-E-E-E-EAR...!!!" he sang with all his might. The toads were truly moved. For as everyone knows toads have highly developed ears for music, and Chadwick's sustained C-sharp moved them into the pond, screaming.

Chadwick huffed, "Riffraff!" Then he left that dreary place to seek admirers elsewhere.

Journeying deeper into the woods behind the village, he soon heard a magical sound of approaching music—of timbrels and flutes and stringed instruments. "What could this be?" he wondered.

Just then a troupe of brightly colored birds of ornate plumage appeared at the crest of a hill, and came at him in a rush of dancing and music.

Chadwick was in awe.

There must have been a half-dozen or more of the beautiful creatures (Chadwick couldn't keep count because they darted about so quickly). One dashed into a hedge and two dashed out. Two flushed up into a tree, and three flushed back. They rushed all about him, playing their instruments loudly and sweeping him along with their wild dancing.

Never had Chadwick heard such musical cheer. Never had he been so carried away by such a jolly crowd.

It was a moving—

PA-A-A-A-R-R-TY!

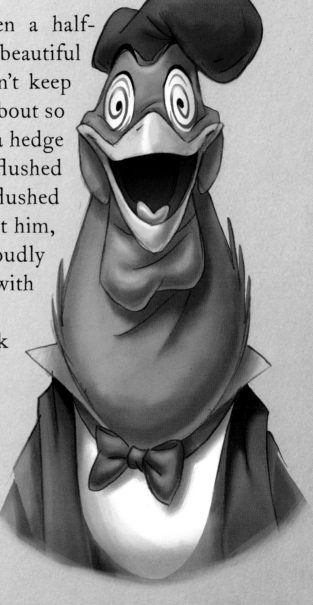

And feathers! Such beautiful feathers! Colors and tails of unimaginable hue and length—of reds and blues and yellows and oranges and purples and white-ringed necks. They each wore fabulous hats adorned with feathers and plumes, and they took his breath away.

"What are you?" Chadwick asked.

"Why, we're a troupe of pheasants," one replied in a rush of yellow.

"Pheasants?"

"Musicians, if you please," another one said in a colorful blur of rust.

"What beautiful feathers you have," Chadwick said.

"Nay, but you have the most beautiful feathers," a pheasant returned, then plucked one from Chadwick's tail and stuck it in his cap.

Chadwick didn't mind at all.

"My name is Chadwick," he said proudly. "I'm a singer of songs."

"A singer of songs!? HURRAY!" the pheasants shouted. They slapped his back. "Why, you're our friend for LIFE!"

Chadwick was delighted. "I am?"

"You ARE!"

And at once the music blazed full volume. The happy troupe swept Chadwick along the road, deeper and deeper into the forest. Unlike the toads, and unlike the animals in Theo's barnyard, they loved his songs. Never had they heard such a voice. They asked him time and again to compose a song to whatever struck their fancy.

"Sing a ditty, and make it witty."
"Write a jingle, and make us tingle!"
Chadwick could hardly keep up with the requests.
With each song the pheasants cheered. "More, more!
Bravo, bravo! We love you, Chadwick, we really do!"

Chadwick's voice became hoarse from all his singing; he ached from all the backslapping. By now his tail feathers were plucked down to the nubs, and decorated each of their hats.

Still, day after day the party went on, night after night it raged; until, alas, Chadwick's voice was gone. And then just as suddenly as the pheasants appeared, they disappeared in three bunches, leaving Chadwick in a ditch.

Chadwick lay there dazed and dizzy for the longest time, wondering what had become of his friends. Had they been real? Were they but a dream? And then he was very lonely.

The proud rooster shuffled away, beaten and bruised and just plain worn out. With his tail feathers plucked there was nothing to crow about now. In fact, he could not utter a squeak, let alone a squawk. Gone was the swank, gone was the swagger, his head hung low as he wandered down the lonely lane, confused and terribly lost.

Chadwick was a very unhappy rooster.

As the sun began to set he found a farmer's pigsty and paused to lick his wounds. He perched atop a rickety fence, and watched the pigs oinking and slopping about in the mud as they ate their supper of corn cobs and swill. By now Chadwick was very hungry. How he would love just one kernel of corn. However, none of the pigs offered to share their supper with poor Chadwick. Instead they gave him a snort. Pigs are like that, you see.

"Woe is me," said poor Chadwick with a sigh. "A rooster
can't get
any lower
than
I."

And then he heard a strange sound, rising from the bottom of his heart. A sound he had not heard before. It was a single note. The note became a word, and the word became a still small voice.

"I have done wrong," the voice said. "I have been a proud rooster. I deserve no better than this."

He remembered how wonderful it had been in Theo's barnyard. At least there he ate well among friends. His true friends. And Theo truly cared for him. He was a kind and gentle man, who gave him a proper coop in which to roost.

"I shall go back and ask their forgiveness," Chadwick said. "I will be a proud rooster no more." And so, early the next morning, long before sunrise, Chadwick started back for home, a tailless, hungry, and very humble rooster.

Meanwhile, as Theo was fixing the board that Oscar the goat had knocked loose on his barn, Luther and Belfry hopped up onto a nearby post and said, "Look, Theo, isn't that Chadwick coming?"

Theo looked down the lane and, sure enough, it was Chadwick. "Praise be!"

There was something different about Chadwick, though. It was not the proud rooster who had left. This Chadwick's head was bowed humbly, there was no arrogant strut in his steps, his beautiful tail feathers were in tatters.

"What happened to him, Theo?" Belfry asked.

Theo smiled thoughtfully. "Our once-proud rooster has come home at last."

Theo ran and lifted Chadwick in his arms and hugged him.

"But I have done wrong, Theo," Chadwick said with a tear in his eye.

"*Grace*," Theo said.

That single word was all he said. Then he gathered the animals together. "Come, let us celebrate our friend's return! For Chadwick was lost but now he is found."

The animals gathered around Chadwick and told him how much they had missed him. Without his crowing to wake them in the morning, no one could quite get his day going properly.

"Won't you compose a song of celebration?" they asked. "A song of true friends!"

Chadwick was humbled, but inwardly he beamed with true joy.

Aren't you glad we have a loving Heavenly Father who welcomes the repenting sinner home with open arms?

For Further Reading, see Luke 15:11-32

For other Theo books and our DVD titles, please visit your local Christian bookstore or find us online at theopresents.com

A Little Overhill Book™

Whitestone Media